Dog Watch

BOOK THREE

Danger at Snow Hill

Dog Watch

Keeping the town of Pembrook
safe for people and dogs!

Dog Watch

BOOK THREE

WOOF!

Danger at Snow Hill

[signature]
2019

By Mary Casanova
Illustrated by Omar Rayyan

Aladdin Paperbacks
New York London Toronto Sydney

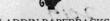

ALADDIN PAPERBACKS
An imprint of Simon & Schuster
Children's Publishing Division
1230 Avenue of the Americas, New York, NY 10020
Text copyright © 2006 by Mary Casanova
Illustrations copyright © 2006 by Omar Rayyan
All rights reserved, including the right of reproduction
in whole or in part in any form.
ALADDIN PAPERBACKS and colophon are trademarks
of Simon & Schuster, Inc.
Designed by Tom Daly
The text of this book was set in Gazette.
Manufactured in the United States of America
First Aladdin Paperbacks edition November 2006
2 4 6 8 10 9 7 5 3 1
Library of Congress Control Number 2005938254
ISBN-13: 978-0-689-86812-2
ISBN-10: 0-689-86812-X

Dedicated to

the dogs of Ranier, Minnesota—
past, present, and future

And

to Kate, Eric, and Charlie—
and to our family dogs, who have
brought us tears and trouble,
laughter and love
over the years

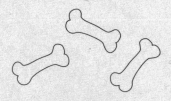

True:

On the edge of a vast northern Minnesota lake sits a quiet little village where dogs are allowed to roam free. Free, that is, until they get in trouble. One report of a tipped garbage can, nonstop barking, or car chasing, and the village clerk thumbs through *DOGGY MUG SHOTS*, identifies the dog from its photo, and places a colorful round sticker on the culprit's page. Then she phones the dog's owner. Too many stickers and the troublesome dog is ordered to stay home—tethered to a chain or locked in its yard. No more roaming, no more adventures with the other dogs of the village.

Sliding Hill Trouble

Snow fell all day in Pembrook. It fell as the village children boarded the yellow school bus in the morning. It fell on the railroad bridge and frosted its rails white. It fell on the big lake and its thin covering of new ice. It fell on the post office, Erickson's Very Fine Grocery Store, Rainy Day Books, the antique shop, and the restaurant. It fell quietly on sidewalks, covering up fresh prints.

All through the day snow fell, tucking the tiny village under a deep white quilt.

And when the school bus returned that late afternoon, the neighbor girls, Emmaline and Zoey, raced home.

Front paws on the window ledge, Kito and Chester watched the girls, and then ran to the back door and whined. In her snowflake slippers and paint-splattered shirt, Mrs. Hollinghorst left her easel. "If it's snowing like this in mid-December, we'll certainly have lots of snow by Christmas. Do you two want to go play in it?" She opened the door and they bolted out.

Since the Tweet family had moved in last fall, everything across the street had changed. The abandoned church had sprouted a swing set outside, curtains inside, and a pinecone wreath on its front door.

In moments, the red-headed sisters bounded out in jackets, snow pants, mittens, and hats. A polka-dot hat tamed half of Emmaline's squirrel-nest hair. Beneath a tossled hat, Zoey's braids hung straight as curtains drawn.

"Kito, Chester! C'mon!" They grabbed

their sleds from the side of the building, then hurried down Pine Street. The dogs jumped and twirled and trotted with them.

Kito couldn't have been happier. He loved the neighbor girls. As he walked, his worries lifted as surely as snowflakes fell. Life with the Hollinghorsts—Mr. and Mrs. H—couldn't be better, and now that it was winter, he didn't have to worry about strangers traveling through and setting his fur on edge. Tourists often didn't understand how village dogs were allowed to run free. But for now, all was well in Pembrook and would stay that way, he hoped, for a good long time.

They crossed Main Street, rounded the corner at the giant spruce, and neared the ice rinks. Beyond the first rink, the wooded hill looked out over village rooftops. Dotted with people and dogs, the sliding hill curved toward them like a white river.

From the smaller rink, where tiny children and parents usually skated, Howie called, "Hi, hi, hi!"

The girls waved back. Chester and Kito wagged their tails.

"Good!" Howie called. "Fwends here!" Then, square as an icebox, steady as a plow, Howie went on shoveling, leaving dark ribbons in his wake. The smaller rink was bordered by snowbanks and benches. Beyond it, the larger rink waited to be cleared for hockey skaters to whack pucks into nets and boards.

"Race you to the top!" Emmaline shouted.

As the girls climbed the hill, a boy threw snowballs at them. "Stop that!" Zoey squealed, and threw snowballs in return.

The sliding hill buzzed. Kids and parents speckled the hill with their saucers and sleds, toboggans and cardboard.

Village dogs chased and tumbled. Lucky, a reliable golden retriever, dashed down the hill despite missing one back leg. Schmitty, though he'd forever be the runt of a black Lab litter, outraced the girls to the top. Good old Schmitty. A smile no matter the day, no matter the weather. Three dogs played chase-the-stick: Tundra, their Dog Watch leader and alpha dog—a white German shepherd who was never without her red bandanna; Gunnar, the only basset hound; and Muffin, a fluffy ball with a pink ribbon at her collar.

While the other dogs played, Kito studied the sign posted at the base of the hill:

KEEP YOUR SLED UNDER CONTROL AT ALL TIMES.
CLIMB ON THE SIDE OF THE SLIDING HILL.
NO SNOWBALL THROWING. . . .

He glanced over his shoulder to make sure no one caught him reading. Too many rules! Snow was meant to be played in. He dove in headfirst, then rolled and rolled until he was a snowman on four legs. "Chow chows were meant for this," he said. He inhaled the damp, clean air and rolled again.

Nearby, Chester dipped his snout beneath the snow's surface. *Snuffle, snuff, snuff.* When he lifted his head, snow covered his nose like whipped cream. "Criminy biscuits!

AKC beagles were most definitely *not* bred for this stuff. I'd take damp leaves and dirt any day!"

At that, Kito charged Chester and tackled him in the deep snow. They wrestled, play-growling and snarling, until they smacked hard into someone's legs.

"Hey!" a woman screeched, skittering back. "Dogs! Knock it off!"

Kito, stung by the woman's stern tone, struggled upright. Her heeled boots left sharp holes in the packed snow. Over her jeans hung a lemon yellow cape embroidered with birds in gold cages. Under the hooded cape, eyes glinted hard as the marbles in Mr. H's glass jar in his writing studio. Kito froze.

The woman wagged her gloved finger at them. "Why do you dogs have to be every-where I turn? I'm going to put an end to this no-leash law in Pembrook if it kills me! I'll see that dogs in this village are leashed—as they should be!"

Kito couldn't believe his ears. A stranger

was threatening their freedom? He bristled and growled a low warning.

"Stop that, you beast!" The woman kicked snow in his eyes. "If I had wanted to live with dogs, I could have moved into a dog kennel where dogs belong, not roaming willy-nilly wherever they please. Now get away! Scram!"

Then she whipped out her camera and began snapping photos—of them!

Blinking, tail between his legs, Kito edged backward to the cover of spruce trees on the hillside. He flopped down in the untouched snow to cool off.

"Criminy cripes—what a crank!" Chester said, following at his side. "But did you need to growl? Now you're really going to be on her list."

"Her *list* is exactly what I'm afraid of. A person like that could ruin everything. I just hope she's passing through to Canada!"

His stomach churned. Everything he loved—the freedom to meet with other dogs at the fire hydrant to exchange news, the freedom to run through the neighborhood, the freedom to swim in the cool, clear lake, and the freedom to race up and down the snow hill—everything was at risk.

Chester cocked his ears. "If she's angry, why did she just take our picture?"

Kito gave his coat a mighty shake, as if to free himself of this new and growing worry. "Maybe to gather evidence. Maybe to make her case against *all* the dogs in our village."

"But why?"

"To get us locked up and leashed like most dogs in the world!"

"Criminy crackers!"

2

Phantom Dog

For several minutes Kito and Chester watched the woman in the yellow cape snap photos of them, the snow-layered trees, and the sliding hill.

Chester snorted. "We better get the word out to Dog Watch."

"Got that right," Kito agreed. "Every dog in Pembrook needs to know not to ruffle the feathers on her coat!" He scanned the hillside for their leader, but Tundra must have already headed to her home above the grocery store. No matter the danger at hand, dogs always knew when it was time to eat.

Kito returned to studying the woman. "The less trouble we have with that green-eyed monster, the better for all of us. That means we all need to be on our best behavior. Besides, I know I can't afford to get another sticker. One more and—"

"I've heard it a jillion times," Chester said. "I know, I know. You'd be locked up forever. But you'd still be fed, y'know."

"Maybe food is enough for you, Chester, but for me food comes second to freedom. There's nothing I want more. To have freedom and lose it would be tragic, beyond bearable, beyond—"

From the woods on the hill above them, came a cry. "Mom! Help!"

Shooting straight at them through the birch trees was a runaway sled. A half second before it struck them, Kito and Chester flung themselves out of the sled's path. It stopped abruptly in the indented snow where they'd just been standing.

"Good gravy!" Chester exclaimed.

At their feet spilled a crying giant blue marshmallow. The boy—no more than six—had landed facedown in the snow. "Mommy!" the little boy cried. "Mommy!"

Kito recognized the boy from around the village. Lumbering toward them, the boy's mother charged like an angry moose. She scooped her child into her capable arms, though he truly was too big to be carried. "I told you, Petey, not to slide through the trees. Did you hit a tree, sweetie?"

Snow melted on Petey's round, reddened face, and a drop of blood dotted his lower lip.

"Noooo!" he wailed. "A d-dog tackled me!"

Villagers drew closer, including the woman with the yellow cape and camera.

"Attacked you?" pressed the boy's mother. "Which dog, Petey?" She lowered her head slightly toward Kito and Chester, as if to charge. "Which dog? Show me. That dog?" She pointed at Kito.

The woman in the embroidered yellow cape loomed closer with her camera, aiming and clicking—at the sled, the dogs, the boy—and zoomed in on the boy's face.

"Nooooo—a different dog!"

Emmaline and Zoey ran down the sliding hill toward them.

"Was it Lucky?" the mother asked her son, whose lower lip appeared to be growing in size.

The boy shook his head.

"Tundra . . . Schmitty, perhaps?"

Again Petey shook his head. "It was a big, black dog!" He touched his mittened hand to his mouth, pulled it away, and looked at the pencil-eraser-size drop of blood. Then he wailed harder.

"Are you sure it wasn't Kito? He's reddish gold, medium in size. . . . Are you sure?"

Click. Click. Click. The stranger took photo after photo. Then she stopped and put her green-gloved hand on the mother's shoulder. "Excuse me, ma'am, but I'm Angelica Phillips. You and I really must talk about this dog problem! Can we go into the warming house?"

"Absolutely!" Then Petey's mother carried him off with the photographer to the squat red building.

"That was weird," Zoey said, watching the women walk off. "I don't care what they say, you're good dogs." She pulled one errant braid from over her shoulder until it hung parallel with her other braid. Then she patted the dogs' heads.

"You two wouldn't hurt anyone," Emmaline said, dropping to her knees and hugging them. "I know it."

"Huh," Chester said, nudging Kito under his chin. "Let's hope those women know that."

But of course, the girls couldn't hear the dogs' silent language. People thought dogs only talked through barks, howls, and whines. But they could also talk with no sounds at all.

Zoey flopped back in the snow. "That Petey tells tall tales," she said, flapping her arms and legs in the snow. "I bet he made the whole thing up."

"Yeah," Emmaline added, shaking her red hair free of snowflakes. "Like the time he got on the bus and said he'd been captured by aliens. I don't think that really happened, do you, Zoey?" She looked up at her older sister.

"'Course not." Zoey jumped to her feet and examined her snow angel with a smile. "Perfect!"

Emmaline frowned. "Or the time he said there were wolves in his backyard. That didn't happen. I'm sure it didn't. Did it, Zoey?"

"Well," Zoey said, dusting off her snow pants and sled, "wolves live all around here. But I don't think one would come right into Pembrook."

"Oh." Emmaline let out a big breath. "That's good." Then she hugged Kito, as if for reassurance.

"Emmie, we better get home for dinner. After we eat, let's come back!"

Kito usually loved evenings at the snowy hill, when a spotlight lit up the slope. The girls gathered their sleds and headed home, with Kito and Chester following. Wood smoke spiced the air. Snow lay like countless stars beneath the streetlights, and as the girls walked, it fluffed in sparkling clouds around their boots.

Kito wished he could enjoy the walk home, but his back twitched with worry. "That Angelica Phillips," he said, "she was awfully serious about getting those photos."

"Yeah," Chester agreed, "she had that camera right in Petey's face—and ours! She gives me the heebie-jeebies."

As they neared their house, Emmaline sped up and glanced over her shoulder. "But what if one was really hungry?" she asked, tugging on Zoey's jacket.

"One what?" Zoey said.

"Wolf!"

Kito's and Chester's ears perked up. They shot each other a wide-eyed look.

Emmaline pressed on. "What if a wolf was really, really hungry?"

"Hmmm. I don't think one would show up

in Pembrook, but, well . . . let's ask Dad."

Emmaline grabbed Zoey's arm. "Maybe a big, black, very, very hungry wolf . . . maybe a wolf like that would come into Pembrook. . . ." Then, without a word, the girls ran to their house.

Chester's eyes widened to white. "Wolves?"

Kito glanced over his shoulder into the darkness. The likelihood that a wolf had entered the village was slim, but it didn't matter. His back hairs stood on end, his heart raced, and his legs gathered in motion beneath him.

As one, Kito and Chester ran to their side of the street, and then skidded across the landing. Surrounded by the glow of Christmas lights, they pawed like crazy on their back door until it finally swung open.

3

Never Cry Wolf?

In the middle of the night, the Christmas tree shimmered with bows, ornaments, and tiny lights of blue, green, red, and violet. In its glow, Kito studied a book on the floor and turned the pages with his paw. He tried to be quiet as a midnight mole. The last thing he needed was to have Mr. or Mrs. H wake up and find him reading. If that ever happened, he could become a circus act. He wasn't worried that Chester would catch him. His beagle buddy was snoring upstairs in bed with the Hollinghorsts.

The book he'd found, *Wolves in the Wild*, stated: "On occasion, a wolf will attack and kill a domesticated dog. One such case happened in northern Minnesota, where a dog was pulled from its doghouse. Attacks on dogs do not appear to be motivated by hunger, but rather by a need for wolves to protect their territory."

Kito shuddered. Wolves attacking dogs? Could this be possible? He thought of Petey's claim that a big dog had injured him, but what if it had been a wolf? Maybe a wolf was lurking in the trees by the hill, eyeing Pembrook dogs with the aim of getting rid of them.

He tried reading further, but his eyes blurred. Carefully, he closed the book with his paw and carried it gently in his teeth to the bookcase. Thank goodness it was on a lower shelf where he'd been able to find it. But his research hadn't made him feel better—only worse.

Curling up by the Christmas tree, he tried to listen hard for the howling song of a nearby wolf . . . but all he heard was Chester's snoring. Zzzzz . . . zzzzz . . . zzzzz . . .

The next morning Mrs. Hollinghorst woke Kito with Christmas music on the piano. "Hey, sleepyhead . . . time to wake up."

Kito rose to his legs and stretched—back arched and head down—and then he stepped to Mrs. H.

Chester sat beside her on the piano bench. He wagged his tail and held his head high.

"Ready to sing?" she asked.

He wagged his tail all the harder.

Kito wasn't much for singing, but he loved the month of December, when Christmas carols filled the house. He loved going with the Hollinghorsts to the village Christmas party at the warming house, when everyone gathered for cookies and cider, sliding and skating. He loved the lights and the way villagers were at their friendliest. This was one time of year when he didn't want to be locked up or kept on a short leash.

On cue, Chester sat right beside the

black upright piano, tilted his head back, and began to sing along. "Wooo—wooo—wooo! Wooo— wooo—wooo! Wooo—wooo— woooooo—wooo—wooo!"

"That's right, Chester!" Mr. H exclaimed, joining them. "'Jingle Bells'! You're getting it!"

With a tingle in his paws, Kito remembered yesterday's events. The threats by Angelica Phillips . . . her photographs . . . Petey . . . and the girls talking about wolves. . . . He couldn't quite sort it all out in his head. It was like a blizzard heading his way. He could sense it coming but could do nothing to stop it.

Before they finished, Kito trotted to the back door and scratched. Finally, Mr. H let him out. At the creaking of the door, Chester raced out on Kito's heels.

"Your singing is fine," Kito said as they explored the snowy edges of their yard and marked their borders. "But we have work

21

to do. Did you forget? We need to put Dog Watch on alert!"

"That's right, that's right!" Chester said. He—*snuff-snuff*—snuffled in the snow. "A mouse . . . somewhere through here last night."

"Mice are the least of our worries right now," Kito said. He huffed. "What are mice compared to wolves?"

Chester lifted his head, a puff of white on his nose. He shook his head and the snow went flying. "Wolves . . . I know Emmaline and Zoey were scared, but you don't really think . . ."

"I don't know what to think. Let's head to the fire hydrant, then investigate the sliding hill. Something was lurking in those trees. I'm not saying it was a wolf, I'm just—"

"But you said 'wolf.' If you're not worried about a wolf, then why did you even mention it?"

"Sometimes, Chester . . . sometimes . . . oh, forget it. Just follow me, please."

The List

Just as the dogs' paws touched Pine Street, Emmaline and Zoey ran from their home across the street.

"Kito! Chester!" Zoey called. "Want to come along?" Her red braids hung neatly beneath her hat and over her powder blue snowsuit.

Kito wagged his tail. "Wish we could," he said, but of course they didn't hear his words.

"Got that right," Chester added beside him. "We have serious business."

Kito liked the girls. It was their cat he

couldn't stand. He scanned Zoey's snowy path from her home. To his great relief, he didn't see their fierce black cat, Sheeba.

As usual, Emmaline's hair was wild as weeds. Most dogs couldn't get away with a mane like that, but Emmaline could. Snowball and Chocolate—the two curly-haired puppies the Tweets had adopted—tripped around Emmaline's boots.

"Brace yourself," Kito said.

"Got that right," Chester answered. "Those pups are a pawful of trouble."

In seconds the puppies were at Kito's and Chester's chins, licking like crazy, asking to be accepted. Kito turned his shoulder. Chester did the same, and they made the puppies follow them. If they were too friendly, they'd be licked to death. Besides, in Pembrook, Tundra was at the top and new puppies were definitely at the bottom. That's just the way it was. They were from the litter of puppies that they'd helped find only two months back. Now the puppies, a little taller than Chester, frolicked.

"Why we helped save you two," Chester said, "I'll never know. Criminy crackers! You two are enough to drive a beagle crazy! And by the way, where were you yesterday afternoon?"

"The vet," said Chocolate.

"Booster shots—yuck!" said Snowball.

When the girls crossed Main Street toward the sliding hill, Kito and Chester made a quick detour left to the fire hydrant outside the post office. They sniffed around for any reports from the other dogs. The fire hydrant, painted by Mr. Cutler to resemble Raggedy Ann, wore a cap of white snow and was surrounded by yellow—and several village dogs.

Villagers carried packages to and from the building, greeting one another with "Merry Christmas!" and "Happy Holidays!" When villagers showed up in numbers, so did the dogs.

Muffin sported a pink turtleneck sweater with candy canes. "What do y'all think?" she asked, twirling around on her hind legs.

"You look like an ornament," Schmitty said, cocking his black Lab head. "Cute."

"Warm," Chester said, shaking. "I wish I had a sweater like that. I mean, not pink of course, but something British. A sporty plaid, perhaps. . . ."

While the dogs chitchatted, Kito walked to Tundra's side. "Reporting in," he said.

Tundra held her head high, showing her top-dog rank.

As Kito told her about the worrisome events at the sliding hill, she sat on her haunches, listening. He knew his place in the

pack. Second-in-command was just fine with him. Sure, on occasion he'd been forced to take the lead, but only when Tundra wasn't around. If he ever tried to take over, she'd have him pinned to the ground, teeth to neck, reminding him who was in charge.

When Kito finished with his news, Tundra rose and circled the other dogs.

"Listen up," she said, walking around the fire hydrant and the dogs clustered around it. Respectfully, the dogs sat: Schmitty, Muffin, Lucky, Gunnar, Chester, and Kito. Chocolate and Snowball, however, being the puppies they still were, kept tumbling about, unable to sit still.

"It has come to my attention," Tundra continued, "that we have two possible threats in our village. The first," she said, "is the possibility of a wolf."

"A wolf!" Muffin blurted. From her tiny nose to her tiny tail, her whole body began to tremble. "My, but I'd be a mere morsel in the mouth of a wolf."

"Plum cake," Chester whispered, sidling

27

up to her, "don't you worry. We'll get to the bottom of this."

"Wolves," Tundra went on, "though they may be our distant relatives, are no friends to domesticated dogs."

"Doooo-mest-*what*?" Gunnar said. He blinked, obviously confused.

"Domesticated," Tundra repeated. "Descendants of wolves. Pet dogs. Tame dogs."

"Ooooh, yeah." Gunnar shifted, then added, "I kneeew that."

"The second threat," Tundra said, "is to our freedom. We must be on our best behavior due to a stranger named Angelica Phillips."

"Who?" Schmitty said. "I've never heard of her."

"But you've seen her," Kito said. "Yesterday, at the sliding hill, remember the woman with the camera?"

"Yeah, but what's wrong with taking pictures?" Schmitty asked.

Tundra answered. "Taking photos of dogs and talking about having them leashed up— that's what's wrong."

Noses united, the dogs growled softly in various pitches.

Suddenly, Chester swung his head. "That's her!"

All the dogs spun. The woman walking toward them was the very woman they were talking about. Angelica Phillips kept one eye on the dogs as she veered wide around their hydrant gathering and humphed loudly. Then, with a swoosh of her yellow cape, she climbed the steps to the post office. "This is ridiculous!" she said.

"Straaangers," Gunnar said, "dooon't get maaaail at the pooost office."

"She doesn't look threatenin'," Muffin said. "Right fashionable to me, that's what."

Three seconds after the door closed, it swung wide open again. This time, Mavis the postmaster was shooing Chocolate and Snowball outside with the toe of her shoe.

"Oh no," Kito groaned. "More trouble! The puppies must have sneaked inside behind Angelica Phillips."

"Out, out, out!" Mavis scolded, her face scrunched up like a dried apricot. Hands on her hips, she glowered at the puppies until they were several feet from the entrance steps.

"How dare you piddle in *my* post office?"

Chocolate and Snowball, more loose skin and legs than brains, cowered and slunk toward the other dogs, their tails tucked under their back legs. They stopped in front of Tundra.

"Chocolate. Snowball," Tundra said. "You didn't, did you?"

The puppies rolled on their backs, paws up.

"Have a little dignity," Tundra said. "Up on your feet, you two. But absolutely no more sneaking inside the post office."

Angelica Phillips stepped out and stood beside Mavis.

"There's no need to put up with this, Mavis," she said, pulling out a spiral note-book from her shoulder bag. She held up a pen. "If you're fed up with dogs sneaking into your post office, tired of them gathering like pesky flies here on the corner, just sign here."

Kito froze. Things were moving toward disaster more quickly than he'd dreamed possible. He glanced at Tundra.

Tundra's tail went up, straight as a flagpole. "Listen up," she said, "Kito was right. We have a serious problem on our paws. All dogs must be on their best behavior. Spread the word—and fast—to all village canines."

Before Angelica Phillips could make any more complaints about the dogs of Pembrook, Tundra barked, "Clear out! To snow hill!"

Kito and Chester took off with the other dogs. Not even the puppies dared stay behind. As they ran, they all broke into a loud, determined chorus: "Morning or night, Pembrook dogs unite!"

5

Tracks of the Intruder

Yipping and barking, the dogs rounded the towering spruce. They turned the corner so fast that several dogs skidded and slipped on the snow-packed road. Something ahead looked wrong.

Outside the warming house, Howie, the rink caretaker, was on his hands and knees. Garbage was scattered around him as if a tornado had struck.

"He must be hurt!" Kito said, speeding up and zipping ahead of the others. What could possibly have happened to his friend Howie? Was he sick? Injured?

Tears flowed down Howie's big, square face. "So much tubble, so much tubble here. Howie lose his job fo' sure."

All around Howie were bits of paper plates, napkins, foam cups, and icy spills of colorful drinks. He was trying to stuff everything into a large plastic garbage bag. The door to the warming house was wide open, and Kito stepped inside. The same disaster covered the cement floor from wall to wall and under every bench. Someone—or something—had caused Howie a huge amount of work. He sniffed the floor. Some dog—some animal—had been there. But who? What?

Kito stepped back outside again as the other dogs sniffed through the garbage, some finding last bits of pepperoni, cheese, and pizza crusts.

"This is great!" called Chester. "So many

wonderful smells!" He—*snuff-snuff*—snuffled with abandon.

Howie kept picking up the garbage and stuffing it into the garbage bag. "I fo'got to shut the door hard last night. This morning—look!" He shook his head. "No good, no good. Howie lose his job fo' sure."

Kito wanted to tell his friend that it would be all right, but all he could do was snuggle his nose under Howie's big arm. Howie patted Kito's head. "It's okay, Kito. Okay."

Suddenly, Kito turned toward a dreaded noise. *Click, click, click, click, click.* He didn't dare look up to see who had arrived. When he did, a camera snapped right in his face.

"I knew it!" Angelica Phillips said. "I knew I wouldn't have to wait long to get more dirt on you dogs. Soon I'll have enough to lock you all away. And enough for a newspaper article, too!"

Wearing white leather gloves, she drew out her pen and notebook. "Um, sir," she said to Howie. "Can you tell me what happened here?"

"Bad tubble," Howie said, then started to cry. "I lose my job fo' sure."

"Did dogs do this? Is that why there's such a mess here?"

Howie shook his head back and forth, then up and down. "Big mess, fo' sure. Last night, big, big hockey party. Lots and lots of pizza. I clean up, go home, come back. Unlock door, shovel and shovel rinks, and then—" He looked around. "And this!" He started to cry again.

"Oh brother," Chester said. "He's not going to make this better for us, is he?"

Angelica Phillips clicked more photos of Howie, his tears, and the surrounding dogs, who were busy finding scraps. Finally she snapped her notebook shut. "Well, that should do it for now." Then she turned and walked away.

Kito and Chester trailed behind her at a distance. Angelica Phillips sauntered a short way down the snow-covered street in her yellow cape, leaving her spiked heel marks as she went. She stepped through the picket fence beyond the towering spruce, and then disappeared into a butter yellow house with white shutters.

"Criminy," Chester said.

Kito sighed. "Oh, no. There was a moving van by that house only a few days ago. That means she's not just passing through. She *lives* here."

He should have known. Earlier, he'd seen a sign in the yard that read SOLD. If only she'd been a tourist, then he could have relaxed. Tourists rarely understood the ways of dogs in Pembrook. But if a villager got upset with the dogs, that was a serious matter. People could speak out on anything that bothered them and try to make changes. They could speak out against dogs, but dogs couldn't speak up for themselves.

It wasn't fair.

The only thing they could do was avoid trouble, which was turning out to be impossible. Beyond that, it seemed there was little they could do to change the mind of

Angelica Phillips about Pembrook dogs.

With a sense of urgency, Kito turned with Chester back toward the warming house and the other dogs. He called out, "We must find out who did this!"

"Think it's the work of a wily wolf?" Schmitty asked, a bread stick in his mouth.

"Wolves are smart," Tundra said, surveying the scene. "They wouldn't get this close to humans just for pizza scraps—not when they have miles of wilderness beyond Pembrook filled with rabbits, mice, and deer. No, I don't believe this was the work of a wolf."

"Then whaaaat could it beeeee?" Gunnar shook his head and sent a strand of drool flying across Chester's back.

"Gee, thanks! Have you no breeding?"

Gunnar's eyes dropped. "C'mon. Beeee kind."

Tundra walked wide around the mess. "Look. Paw prints of all sizes and shapes, but they're all ours. For a moment, everyone listen up! Try to forget the pizza smells! Sniff around. What do you smell?"

Chester snorted and snuffled, then lifted his head, eyes wide and nose twitching. "Nope. It's not one of us. But there is too much fresh snow here to determine more than that." He went back to sniffing. *Snuffle, snuff, snuff.* "Yet there's a scent of fear and desperation here."

"Fear. Desperation," Tundra repeated. She looked to Kito.

"Fear can make some animals even more dangerous," Kito said cautiously. "We need to be on guard. If it has attacked a child, it certainly wouldn't be afraid to attack one of us."

Tundra barked out a command. "Every dog, fan out! Gunnar, Schmitty—you two take the north side of the sliding hill."

"But I miiiiight get stuuuuck," Gunnar protested.

"Stuck?" she repeated.

"Myyyyy legs aaaare toooo shoooort."

"Okay, change of plans. Gunnar, Muffin—you two with the shortest legs, you take the warming house. Look for any signs you can find. Unusual hairs, a collar left behind, claw marks . . . If you get on the trail of this intruder, send up a howl."

"I'm fixin' to find the culprit!" Muffin exclaimed, dancing in circles and trembling at the same time.

"Schmitty and Lucky, you two take the north side of the hill. Chester and Kito, you take the south side."

"That's what I was afraid of," Chester said under his breath.

Tundra pounced and landed with a flurry of snow beside Chester. She put her nose to his. Her mouth was large enough to swallow him from snout to ears. "Are you objecting, Chester?"

"No sir, I mean ma'am. I'm right on it, Tundra."

"Good. That's better." Her back hairs settled down and the dogs fanned out.

As Kito and Chester neared the south side of the hill, Chester whined. "I'm scared. This is exactly where we were yesterday when Petey came flying through." He glanced around nervously. Then, like a skater on sharp blades, or like the coward that Chester deep down was, his little legs sped him around the base of the wooded hill toward home.

"Hey, get back here!" Kito called. "Where are you going?"

Despite his best intentions to track down the intruder, Kito suddenly wasn't feeling brave enough to explore the shadowy woods on his own.

Without a backward glance, he took off, too, after Chester.

6

Front-Page News

That afternoon Kito gazed out the door, waiting for Mrs. Buckman to deliver the newspaper. She'd taken over Howie's paper route while he worked at the warming house and rinks for the winter months. Finally her rusty Buick rolled by, slowed at the newspaper box beside the road, and rattled on.

Mr. H tromped outside in his slippers for the paper and returned with it under his arm. Kito had to know if Angelica Phillips had put anything about them in the paper. If she had, it could be the beginning of the end of their freedom. He tried not to shake with anxiousness.

Mr. H plopped in the leather chair beside the woodstove, sighed, and propped his feet on the coffee table.

Kito sat beside him, acting as if he just wanted to be scratched. When Mr. H turned the page, the front-page headline nearly took Kito's breath away: NUISANCE DOGS GROW IN NUMBER.

How could she? True to her word, Angelica Phillips had penned an article complete with photos and captions: One showed Petey crying, with Chester and Kito looking guilty behind him; one showed dogs at the fire hydrant, with a caption that read, "Pack Size Grows Outside Post Office"; and another showed dogs at the warming house, pawing through debris beside Howie. The caption said: "Dogs Create Garbage Disaster."

When Mr. H left the paper and headed up the spiral staircase to his writing studio, Kito scanned the rest of the article quickly. None of it was a surprise, but what sent a chill down his spine were the words at the end of the article: "An emergency meeting to review Pembrook's dog policy is scheduled for seven p.m., December 14. Everyone is strongly encouraged to attend."

This was worse than terrible! The meeting was tomorrow evening. He had little time to inform the dogs, and the dogs had even less time to change their overall bad image. Oh, to be falsely accused without the chance to defend themselves! Where was the justice in that? This could turn out to be the worst Christmas ever. If they lost their freedom, not a single dog would be able to go to the village Christmas party without being on a leash. Worse still, if Angelica Phillips got her way, dogs might be banned from such events completely!

Chester was snoozing on the rug in front of the woodstove. "Psst!" Kito whispered. "Wake up, buddy. This is no time to relax."

Chester's legs began to twitch and run as he lay on his side, his eyes closed. "Don't— don't eat me," he pleaded. "I have papers. . . . yes, I'm a registered beagle. . . ."

"Chester, Chester," Kito said, this time more firmly. "Snap out of it!"

Chester opened one eye, then rose to his legs and stretched. "Just a little nap, that's all."

"Hey, I can't blame you for running off. I mean, I followed right behind you and I'm not proud of it, but that doesn't change our duty. We dropped the bone and left the other dogs out there. We have to get back on the job."

"Criminy biscuits," Chester said. "How are we supposed to hold our heads high now?"

"There's only one way."

"And what's that?"

"Go back."

"You mean— to the sliding hill?"

"That's right." Kito headed to the door and scratched until Mrs. H left her easel and her painting of a rabbit.

"Okay, boys, I hear you."

As soon as their paws touched snow, the dogs bolted through the deepening shadows past houses decorated with lights and Santas, reindeer and angels. Kito filled Chester in on the newspaper article, claiming that Mr. H had read it aloud while Chester was napping.

"That's serious," Chester said. "Scared or not, our only hope is to find the troublemaker and make sure the intruder gets locked up— not the rest of us!"

They bolted around the spruce at the corner, closed in on snow hill and a handful of sledders, then aimed for the hill's wooded southern slope. "This time," Kito said, "we're going to search together. There's safety in numbers."

"Got that right," Chester agreed. "Speaking of numbers, where is everybody?"

"The rest of Dog Watch must have come up

empty-pawed and headed home for dinner."

"Think Tundra's mad at us for running off?"

"Let's hope she thinks we did our job before we headed home."

They edged off the packed snow at the base of the hill and sank deep in the fresh, untrodden snow near the trees.

"You go first," Chester said. "You know, break trail and all that."

Kito pushed ahead. "No problem."

With eyes, ears, nose, and back hairs on full alert, he stepped deeper and deeper into the covering of trees. If the snow hadn't been falling off and on, maybe they could find fresh tracks, but everything was layered in fluffy white. They headed under snowy brambles.

Chester began snuffling, head buried to his shoulders. "Here," he said, lifting his head and holding up a slice of frozen pizza. "Evidence." He lowered his head again, this time coming up with a ham hock bone. "And this. Some creature has been hiding its stash here!"

Kito glanced around. A growl sounded from somewhere. Chester froze in point position: front paw up, tail straight out.

All around in the shadowy grayness, all Kito could see was fresh snow. Then, only a few feet ahead, he glimpsed a snow-topped stump and a hole in the snow. "That hole," he whispered, "must lead to its burrow."

"Oh, my gosh," Chester said. "A bear's den? Maybe bears attack dogs and g-g-get into garbage."

"And sleep in dens," added Kito.

Chester shivered. "Last fall, remember w-w-when garbage cans were spilled around town for a few days?"

Again, a low and throaty rumble rose from the den.

At that, the dogs turned on their toenails in the snow and plowed back so fast that they nearly buried each other. The moment their feet hit the packed snow of the sliding hill, their legs were nearly knocked out from beneath them as a flying saucer slid past.

"Hey, dogs! Watch out!" A man sat cross-legged on the saucer with a bundled toddler in his lap. The saucer veered out of control, tipped over, and sent the man and child tumbling. The man knelt beside his child. "Oh, I'm sorry, baby." A wail rose from the child's snow-covered face.

From halfway up the side of the slope, a familiar voice shot down the hill. "See, Edmund?" Petey's mother shouted to the man. "I'm telling you, go to the meeting. We have to put a stop to this dog trouble! Those dogs could have killed you by stepping into your path like that!"

"Good gravy with dog biscuits!" Chester exclaimed. "We have trouble every way we turn!"

Kito glanced over his shoulder at the woods. If a bear was part of their troubles, he and Chester were going to need help to roust it from its den and send it packing. They were going to need every dog in Pembrook—and every ounce of courage.

7

Flyers, Flyers Everywhere!

The next morning, when Mrs. H donned her lavender parka and matching mukluks, Kito and Chester jumped up and down at her feet.

"Down boys, down," she scolded. "I see you want to walk with me to the grocery store."

They wagged their tails. They loved roaming on their own, but walking with their owners was always the best.

As they passed the post office, Kito looked for Dog Watch members, but no dog was in sight. It was still early. Mavis hadn't opened up yet and the flagpole was bare. Nonetheless, the two dogs zipped across the empty street and left an emergency message at the hydrant for others to find later. Then they caught up again with Mrs. H.

"Soon as we have enough dogs to call a meeting," Kito said, trotting alongside Chester, "we need to run whatever is in that den straight out of town!"

"Right-o," Chester agreed. "I barely slept thinking how we might have a bear on the hill. I mean, the den. Going after food. Attacking little Petey."

"Hmmm, maybe."

"Well, something scared him when he sledded through those trees. Something big, dark, and shaggy—like a bear!"

Kito gave his coat a shake. "I'm not so sure. I mean, bears den up late in the fall. Once they start hibernating, I don't think they wake up easily. We're into winter now."

"Good gravy, Kito! Whatever went after those pizza scraps was too hungry to sleep, that's all. Doesn't mean a bear wouldn't wake up if it smelled fresh, hot, tasty pizza. You know, pepperoni pizza with the cheese melted just so. . . . I can almost smell—"

"Focus, Chester. We know something was growling in that den. And we need to send it packing."

The OPEN sign hung in the window of Erickson's Very Fine Grocery Store. The lights were on, and a wreath decorated the door. Mrs. H stepped inside. "You boys wait here."

They sat their rumps on the sidewalk, just as a snowplow rumbled along the street toward them.

"That thing terrifies me!" Chester waited.

"Well, hang tight, buddy. The last thing you need to do is bolt into its path."

As it neared them, it sent a blizzard of snow into the air and left a drift alongside the road. Kito looked for Chester. He was nowhere to be found. Then a little black nose wiggled from the snowdrift, and out sprang his buddy.

"Fatty food scraps! That was ridiculous. Next time, I'm hightailing it as soon as I hear a snowplow coming!"

Before long, Mrs. H stepped from the store with a grocery bag. "Merry Christmas to you, too!" she called over her shoulder. "Will you be at the village Christmas party, Molly?"

The young woman called back, "Hope to—if I can get the evening off work."

"Well, you tell Mr. Erickson to close up shop and not to be stingy. He needs a little Christmas cheer too!"

"Okay, Mrs. Hollinghorst. I will."

Kito glanced at the counter as the door closed. Molly Mitford was the kind of villager who blended in wherever she went. She seemed to disappear behind her glasses and drab brown hair the same way she spent her life behind the grocery store counter. Kito hoped she would be at the village party. She always gave half of her food to the dogs.

"That's it!" Kito said.

"What?" Chester replied. His snout was

pointed toward Mrs. H's grocery bag as they walked beside her. "Hmmm . . . sliced turkey and provolone cheese . . . I'm certain of it. . . ."

"We need to blend in. If every dog in Pembrook could work at being quiet, barely being seen, like Molly Mitford, maybe we would never have any real threat of getting locked up."

"What planet do you live on?" Chester said, meeting Kito's eyes. "That's never going to happen and you know it. We're dogs, dogs, dogs. Great biscuits! I hate to disagree with you, but nothing is really going to change that simple fact."

"Okay, Mr. Positive, Mr. AKC, so what *can* we change?"

"Get the intruder out of town, remember? That's what we can change."

For once, Kito had to admit, Chester was right.

As they neared the fire hydrant, Chester wagged his tail. Already Muffin, Lucky, Schmitty, and Tundra had gathered. The flag hung high, fluttering against the whitish gray sky, and villagers bustled in and out of the post office.

When Mrs. H stepped in to get her mail, Kito and Chester joined the others at the hydrant.

"A den with a creature inside? Are y'all sure 'bout this?" Muffin asked, giving her head a shake. She wore a new Christmas sweater with gold snowflakes on a red background.

"Not entirely," said Kito.

"Absolutely, positively," Chester stated. "We've got a bear right here in Pembrook."

Schmitty cocked his head. "No kidding?"

Tundra stood tall and circled the other dogs until they were all sitting respectfully and giving her their full attention. "If we know where the troublemaker is, then that's half the battle. Anyone have experience dealing with bears, if indeed that's what we're facing?"

"I'm a registered beagle." Chester stood taller.

A groan went up from the rest of the dogs. "Nothin' we ain't heard before," Muffin said.

"Hear me out," he continued. "From the day I was born, my mother told me about hunts of old, how beagles were bred to go in packs after foxes. Royal hunts. They chased them down until—"

"A bear, remember?" Tundra said. "Not a fox. I don't see your point."

"My point is this," Chester said. "Numbers. One on one, a bear could swipe a dog with its massive paw and turn it into cottage cheese. With numbers—with many dogs—the bear would turn tail and run. It wouldn't want to take on a pack. That's my point."

"Thank you, Chester," said Tundra. "Point well taken."

Just then, Angelica Phillips stepped toward the post office. She gave the dogs a smirky smile. Under her arm she carried a stack of yellow papers. When she turned away from the community bulletin board beside the door, a yellow flyer was posted for all to see:

EMERGENCY MEETING TONIGHT
7:00
AGENDA: DOG PROBLEMS

Kito nearly choked on the words as he read them. He'd read about a meeting in last night's newspaper. But this—actually posting flyers around the village—was doubly serious. He glanced around at the dogs, none of whom showed a bit of concern over the flyer. Of course not. He wished he could tell them, but a dog who could read, well, it was unnatural. The others just wouldn't understand.

Already Angelica Phillips was outside the tavern, tacking up her hateful flyer. And then off she headed, as focused as a worker bee, toward the grocery store and restaurant. Kito watched her, his back hairs bristling.

When Mrs. H stepped out of the post office, she stopped beside the flyer and read it aloud. This time the dogs all pivoted their ears toward her voice.

"Dog problems? Huh. Well that's just

plain ridiculous," she said. She glanced at the dogs. "*What* dog problems?"

If only this threat could be solved by Mrs. H, bless her. But the problem was growing larger by the minute. By the time it reached the ears of villagers at the emergency meeting tonight, Kito worried that it would be too late. Not even the kindhearted Hollinghorsts could go against a majority vote.

Tundra spun back to the dogs. "Split up—you know the drill—and go to every door in Pembrook and call on all dogs. Don't take no for an answer. Tell every dog they're to report at noon today here at the fire hydrant. No slackers, no excuses." She growled to underscore her point. "Got it?"

Kito shot Chester a glance. Tundra's concern could only mean one thing—*she* was worried too. Maybe it really was a bear!

Back hairs ruffled, all the dogs barked and yipped in unison.

8

A Pack of Baying Hounds

Behind the grocery store, Mr. Erickson tossed meat and fat scraps from a cardboard box. Penny, the white-muzzled golden retriever, trotted out the door from Rainy Day Books, just across the street. Chester raced to the feet of Mr. Erickson and begged, watching intently the grocer's every move.

Kito sat beside him. "We're supposed to be getting the word out to this end of the village, not eating!"

"We are," Chester replied, then caught a scrap in his mouth. Between bites he told

Penny about the noon meeting at the fire hydrant.

"I don't move so very fast these days," Penny said. "Please tell Tundra for me that I need my nap." Then she snapped a scrap out of the air with such keenness and expertise that Kito took note.

"That may be," he said, "but you're going to have to tell her yourself."

"Oh. Do you mean it?"

"Yup. Tundra said 'no excuses.' Every dog in the village must be there."

"Penny, Penny," Chester started. "It will be like fox hunts of days gone by."

"I don't remember any fox hunts around Pembrook," she said, "and I'm twelve years old."

"No, not here in Minnesota—I'm talking about England, the land of my ancestors. Stories have been passed down to beagles for generations. Rise early, smell the dew on the morning grass, gather together in chorus . . . mighty fine times those were, with horses and riders following the pack. . . ."

"Chester," Kito said. "Get a grip. Your best hunting experiences have been following the trail from your bed to your dog dish."

Mr. Erickson turned the box upside down, as if to prove his point. "That's it, dogs. More tomorrow." Then he went back into the grocery building.

"Why did Mrs. H call him stingy?" Chester asked.

"He's not stingy with dogs," Penny said, sitting back on her ample haunches, her belly nearly touching the snow. "He's always been willing to share leftovers."

"Well, some people get along better with dogs than with people," Kito said, moving on down the lane. "That's the way it is."

They headed past the house where Spike lived. They called out the news of the meeting to the dog kennel. In seconds, plowing up snow with his four paws, Spike charged full speed at them. When he reached the end of his heavy chain, he stopped in midair and dropped to the ground, growling and showing his teeth. Not only was he a real biter, he was a real fighter, too. Kito and Chester veered away from him.

"Just wanted to let you know," Kito said, "in case you could make it."

Spike let out a rumbly roar of a bark. "'Course I can't be there!"

"He'd eat us for lunch if he could," Chester whispered.

"Phew. I know. But we had to let him know, right?"

After notifying two more dogs beyond the beach, Kito and Chester turned back and spotted Willow outside Woody's Fairly Reliable Guide Service. Woody was busy packing up a snowmobile with gear. Behind it, he trailered a portable icehouse. Willow twirled and whined at her owner's heels.

"No, girl," Woody said. "Can't come along today. Got clients from Chicago I need to help catch some fish."

Willow, with her sleek amber coat and gentle ways, sat down and wagged her tail softly across the top of the snow.

"Look," Chester said. "A tail angel. And it

couldn't have been made by a sweeter dog in all of Pembrook." He sighed. "She's *so* cute."

Kito looked at the fanlike shape in the snow. "Hey, Willow. Heard the news yet?"

But before she could answer, Woody revved the snowmobile engine, and plumes of grayish purple smoke swirled around them. The guide waved, then took off down the snowy shoulder of the road toward the ice covered lake.

"Heard about the meeting, sugar?" Chester asked.

Willow turned to him. "What meeting?"

Chester filled her in. "So if we don't scare the bear out of town, and it keeps causing trouble—"

Kito finished his sentence. He didn't really like that Chester was trying to sound so important in front of Willow. "Then the trouble will fall on all of us dogs."

"How so?" she asked.

"Sweet cake," Chester said with a shake of his coat. "Haven't you been keeping up on anything?"

"Angelica Phillips," Kito said. "The emergency meeting tonight."

Willow looked at him and blinked, her dark eyes and thick lashes nearly knocking Kito off his paws. He tried to keep his mind on their mission. "The, um, er, long and short of it," he said, "is meet at the fire hydrant at noon. Tundra is taking no excuses."

Willow scratched under her collar with her hind foot. "But how do I know when it's noon?"

Chester cocked his head. "Sugarplum, it's real soon. Don't you even know how to tell time?"

She looked down at her paws.

"Come here." He trotted to the front steps of the grocery store, with Kito and Willow following. Above the entry door hung a large, round clock. "First it has to be daytime. You know, light outside."

"Okay."

"Then, when the small hand and the big hand are both straight up—that's noon."

"But what about the other times of the

day?" she asked. "How do you tell those?"

"What?" Chester asked, surprised by her question. "Noon is the only time there is. All dogs know when it's noon."

"And some know when it's midnight, too," Kito added. "But you have to be awake late at night to know that one."

Chester was busy watching the clock. "Almost, almost," he said. "Okay! Tallyho!" He lifted his chin, rounded his pointy beagle snout, and sent up a wail. "It's noon. We'd better skedaddle down to the hydrant."

At that the dogs raced side by side toward the post office.

Sure enough, every dog except Spike was there within seconds. Kito had never seen such a turnout. By quick count, he figured nineteen dogs—no, with Snowball and Chocolate, twenty-one. Amazing. Dog Watch in action! His heart filled with pride that they had become so organized in their effort to work toward keeping the village safe for humans and dogs.

Tundra strode, head high, around the dogs. They all sat respectfully as she neared. "We will roust the bear from Pembrook!" she ordered.

A flurry of yips rose to meet with ice crystals in the air.

"Chester," she said, "I think that perhaps you were called to lead this mission with that nose of yours."

Kito nudged him. "Hey, almost like Rudolph, right, little buddy?"

"Not funny," Chester whispered. "This is real life, not just a story!"

And then, within seconds, Chester turned his nose to the snowy pavement. Straight as an arrow, he shot out ahead of the dogs, baying at full volume. The rest of the dogs took up his chorus.

"Tallyhoooooooo!" Chester wailed.

The Deep, Dark Den

The pack of twenty-one dogs rounded the icy bend in the road, skidding, slipping, and flying out of control. Soon, gathered again in pack formation, they headed toward the south side of the sliding hill. They needed to stay focused and run the bear out of town. Then, Kito figured, he could relax.

"For the love of England!" Chester called, baying at a high pitch. "Onward to knighthood! Tallyhooooo!"

"Knighthood?" Schmitty said to Kito,

with a shake of his floppy black Lab ears. "England? He's losing it."

The dogs passed the smaller skating rink, where a class of young skaters in pink tutus whirled and twirled around on the ice. At the hockey rink beyond, a hockey team practiced and slammed pucks—*crack, whack, smack*—into the rink boards. Howie stood between the rinks, resting against the handle of his shovel and smiling as the dogs neared.

"Hi, hi, hi!" he called to the dogs, but they didn't turn from their course.

They ran across the base of the sliding hill, risking their lives as sleds and saucers zoomed down. The mild temperature had brought out dozens of kids and parents.

"Watch it!" shouted a young man.

"Hey, dogs—look out!" called another.

A shrill, familiar voice met Kito's ears. He glanced over his shoulder, but he didn't slow his stride. It was Angelica Phillips, this time sporting a bright yellow hooded parka and shaggy boots. "I wish those dogs could read the sign now!"

Kito stopped abruptly and looked back. The sign on the edge of the hill had been altered. Another rule had been added in black letters: NO DOGS ALLOWED!

He wished she'd never moved to town. Angelica Phillips was quickly ruining everything good about being a village dog.

The pack was barking ahead of him, with Chester baying in the lead. Kito turned from the sign and hurried to catch up. Moving a sleeping bear could be dangerous, deadly work. Dog Watch needed to stick together more than ever before. He'd overheard a story at the post office once, about a country dog that had tried to run a bear out of its farmyard, only to have the bear swipe him

down—dead—with its massive paw. "Claws sharp and long as nails," the man had said.

Kito shuddered. He plowed through the deep snow after the other dogs, winding his way among aspen, balsam, and spruce. He passed by Lucky and Penny, the two golden retrievers, and Gunnar and Muffin, whose heads barely cleared the snow top. The puppies were stuck in a drift, trying to wiggle themselves free.

"Keep working at it," Kito said. "I'll come back and help you later if you're still stuck."

Deeper into the trees the pack pushed, and finally they stopped by the snow-topped stump. Beside it was a small, dark opening, from which came a low, menacing growl.

"Stand firm," Tundra said, her back hairs

at attention, and blending in perfectly with the snow, except for her red bandanna.

"So, how are we fixin' to get the bear out?" Muffin asked, her voice quaking.

"This is sca-a-a-a-ary," Gunnar added.

"This is no time to lose our nerve," Tundra said. "Kito—come forward."

Kito's heart thudded with dread.

"We need to force the bear out. And I believe you're the right dog for the job."

Kito inhaled a big breath of air. Tundra was right. Being part chow chow, he had the breeding to be brave, to be fearless, to stare down danger and not run away. Maybe his ancestors did just that when they guarded the emperors of China, but he trembled. His tail started to droop, and he had to force it up and into the stately curl over his back. Couldn't he just refuse? Run home?

"Put my head into the den? Is that what you're asking?"

Her eyes met his. "Yes."

All the dogs were silent.

Kito stepped closer to the den's entrance.

He smelled the odor of an animal that had never had a bath. An animal that foraged on garbage rather than living off berries and such from the wild. An animal that had likely attacked a boy on his sled. Kito paused—long enough that snow melted under his pads—and finally willed himself to step closer.

From within the den the growling sounded again, this time louder, and wickedly menacing. This bear did not want to be disturbed. "Maybe," Kito whispered, "we could let it sleep until spring?"

"Between now and then," Tundra said, "who knows how much worse the animal might make things for dogs? More garbage raids, more attacks? And we'd be blamed."

"I know," he said, "you're right." He had to act, even if it cost him his one and only precious life.

He started to dig at the snowy entrance. Snow flew from his front feet to his back legs, and he kicked it out behind him with fury. With each thrust of his back legs, he grew stronger. Braver.

The growling within built into a low-throated rumble.

Kito expected his life to be over any second, but so be it. If he was attacked, the other dogs would then pounce on the culprit. His life would be celebrated for years to come. He'd be nothing short of a hero.

With increasing determination, he dug. Soon the hole was plenty wide enough so he could crawl in. Every hair on his body bristled. He yapped and snapped as he entered the den.

The dogs behind picked up the chorus, barking and cheering him on.

Beneath his paws snow gave way to earth. Smells of autumn leaves, black dirt, and pizza met his nose. On his belly, he crawled in deeper, crawled over several sharp bones, crawled in until he thought he would die from fear.

And then he utterly froze— when his wet, cold nose met up with *another* nose.

10

Big, Black, and Burly

Darkness made it impossible to see the animal before him, but one thing was certain: Kito was sure he'd met his end. He backed up from the dry, hot nose. His own tail was tucked so tightly under his back legs that he tripped.

"Wait," the animal said in a raspy, pained voice.

What? Only dogs could understand the language of dogs. And this bear—this creature—had spoken. That could only mean . . . it wasn't a bear, or a wolf, or anything of the sort. It was a dog!

Visions of Spike—sharp teeth and scraggly coat—flashed through Kito's mind. Dogs could be just as vicious as any bear. He continued edging backward toward the opening. What was a dog doing in a den and causing problems in the village? Kito stopped. He wasn't the one who needed to leave. It was the intruding dog.

"You're not wanted here," Kito said into the darkness. "We've come to chase you out."

The bulky shadow shifted. "I'm not . . . wanted . . . anywhere."

"Who—who are you? Why are you causing us trouble?"

The dog drew a deep, ragged breath. Was he going to attack? After all, Kito had intruded into his home, no matter how primitive it seemed. Any dog would defend the place where he slept.

"Go. Leave me . . . to die."

"To die? There's no reason you need to die. You need to get out of here, that's all.

Nobody is talking about dying. The problem is that you're living right in the middle of Pembrook, and threatening the freedom of all the dogs in this village. You can't just hole up here in this den."

The dog didn't answer, making Kito restless. Nothing about this dog felt normal. He gave Kito the creeps. "Well, uh, it's warmer than I would have guessed in here," he said. "Cozy in its own way."

Still no word from the intruder.

"Just come out," Kito said, with a little more courage. "Step out and tell all the dogs of the village who you are and what you aim to do. That's not asking too much."

"Aim . . . to do?" the dog repeated, his voice deep.

"Right. Aim to do. You know, like move on to another village, get out of town, go back home. . . ."

"I . . . have no home that I . . . can remember."

Scrape, slide, *huff*. The dog slunk closer. Scrape, slide, *huff*.

Kito's top coat bristled. Was this a monster dog, a freakish creature like ones he'd read about in *Dracula* and *Frankenstein*? He trembled, ready to bolt and be done with this dark business.

When the dog was closer to Kito, his condition became clear. He was a huge, shaggy, black Newfoundland, and he lay on his side with a gaping, nasty wound. No wonder he had to pull himself along. He was too injured to stand or walk.

"You're hurt! What happened to you?"

Now that the dog had pulled himself closer, he closed his eyes, as if everything in the past few moments had taken the last drop of his energy. His massive head lay right at Kito's feet. He was as big as a bear cub, with paws bigger than any dog's in the village. The wound in his side was raw and red.

"What are you doing here? You need to get to a vet!"

The Newfoundland raised his head with a groan, then dropped it to the earth floor again.

Outside, the other dogs began to bark. Tundra's voice rose above the pack's. "Kito! Are you okay in there? Should I come in?"

"No, no," he called back. "I'm fine!"

"Is the bear sleeping? Be careful! It could wake again."

"I wish it were a bear," Kito called. "But our problem is much bigger than that."

"Oh, sweet honey," Muffin cried. "Bigger than a bear? I ain't stickin' around to find out!"

At that, cries of "I'm out of here!" "Bigger than a bear!" and "Time for dinner!" rang out from the dogs. And in an instant, the barking outside stopped.

"Get back here!" commanded Tundra. "We need to work as a team, remember?"

Kito turned his attention back to the dog at his feet. "What's your name? How did you get here?"

But the big, shaggy, bearlike dog didn't answer. Kito touched the dog's nose for the second time with his own. He should have figured it out the first time they'd touched noses. The dog was burning up with fever. Kito grabbed him by the ruff of his neck without puncturing the dog's skin. He pulled at the heavy weight, but the dog barely budged.

"Come on," he said. "You have to get up. You can't stay in here the way you are. If you can make it to my home, my owners—they're good people—I'm sure they'll see that you get some help."

The dog growled but didn't open his eyes.

Kito turned and stuck his head outside.

Only two feet away, Tundra paced back and forth in the deep snow. "Worthless team of losers!" she said. "Slackers! They all ran away. Before we can accomplish anything, I need to remind them who's in charge around here." Then she bolted away from the den, leaving Kito behind.

"Wait!" Kito called. "There's a dog hurt in here that needs our help!" But she was out of earshot, and the snow seemed to swallow his words. "Dog Watch." He moaned. "Why did I ever think it could be a good idea?"

Kito crawled back into the den and again tried to pull at the limp and lifeless dog, but the dog didn't budge more than a paw-width. Kito tried yet again, and fell back with a thud on his haunches. His eyes adjusted gradually to the darkness.

"Listen, I can't pull you out," he said. "And everyone abandoned me. So either you get up and walk—or you're probably going to die here!" He hoped his words would roust the dog, whose breathing had grown shallow. Though the dog was large, its ribs protruded as he lay on his side.

"I'll be back," Kito said, "with some food. I promise." Then, though reluctant to leave, he took off through the woods. How quickly life could change. He'd come to get rid of a village menace, and now he was figuring out how to help an injured, homeless dog.

11

Feeding the Hungry

When Kito emerged from the woods at snow hill, he was the only dog around. Sliders sledded and skaters skated on. Angelica Phillips, arms crossed over her parka, talked with Petey's mother. Not a single dog could be found. Not even Chester had waited for him! His shoulders drooped. He needed to talk with someone—especially Tundra—about what to do next. He felt abandoned and let down.

Alone, he trotted home on snowy streets.

Chester met him the moment Mrs. H opened the door.

"What did you find? Did you get hurt, you

know, clawed or chewed? If you did, maybe Tundra could knight you—just like the Queen of England rewarded knights of old. She probably rewarded hounds that were extra brave too."

"Huh. I doubt that. And I doubt Tundra would care whether I was brave. *She* didn't even stick around for me."

"She didn't?"

Kito followed Chester to the woodstove and flopped down two feet away from it. Tongues of fire leaped in the stove, crackling and flickering blue, yellow, and orange. Kito sighed. "*Everyone* took off."

Chester watched the flames, wordless for a rare moment.

"I didn't mean to take off," Chester finally said, rather lamely. "But when Muffin went crazy, her panic sent chills through me, and the other dogs started backing away . . . and before I knew it, I was running away with the rest of them. And suddenly, all I could think of was, well, food."

"Food. I could have been in that den with a

bear. I could have been scraped and chewed up!"

Chester tucked his head between his outstretched paws. His forehead twitched with worry lines. "I'm sorry. I shouldn't have run off on you. I'm really, really, really sorry. Criminy! I feel bad. What was I thinking? We're pals. We stick together."

Kito let Chester's words ease his hurt. How could he stay mad at his friend now? "Okay, I accept your apology. But nobody's going to knight you for running off," he said, closing his eyes. And before he knew it, he was fast asleep.

When he woke, Mr. H was sitting in the leather chair, reading the newspaper. Kito rose, stretched, then ambled closer for a scratch—and a chance to catch up on the news.

In full color, covering the top half of the front page, was a photo of dogs. The Pembrook dogs had been captured on film at the sliding hill, running out of the woods as a pack. The headline read: PACK WORRIES RESIDENTS.

"Honey," Mrs. H called over her shoulder from her easel. "Are you going with me to the meeting?"

"Oh, I suppose. Somebody needs to stand up for the dogs."

"But running as a huge pack. That's not good. I don't know what to think."

Kito wanted to think about only good things. The lights, the dazzling tree, going to the village Christmas party soon—but his mind spun back to the dog in the den.

After dinner, Kito managed to sneak a few chunks of beef from the leftover stew. He carried them carefully in his mouth. Then, when Mr. and Mrs. H left for the emergency dog meeting, Kito trotted past the lit-up community building toward the sliding hill.

"Just tell me," Chester said, staying at his side. "What are you up to?"

But Kito didn't answer. He carried the

beef chunks silently. Chester could follow if he wanted to, but if not, he'd do this on his own. There was a dog that needed help, and he had to reach out. No dog deserved to be hungry, or homeless, or injured. With Christmas coming, he felt it in his bones all the more that he had to do what he could.

For all he knew, the dog might be dead by now.

Like a giant lantern, the full moon lit up the village and woods. Chester badgered Kito with questions the whole way. When Kito trudged through the deep snow toward the den, Chester balked. "No way, no way," he said. "I'm not going there."

Kito kept going. When he looked back, Chester had fallen a few steps behind, but at least he was following.

Moonlight shimmered across the snow and sent a faint glow into the den. Kito crawled right in. To his relief, the dog was breathing. "You came . . . back?" the dog managed.

Kito dropped the beef chunks right before the Newfoundland's nose. "Yup. Can't just leave you here, hungry and hurt."

Without rising to his legs, the big dog snapped up the food until it was gone. "Nobody has ever . . ."

Chester snuffled in. "Where's the big bear?"

"There is no bear," Kito explained, "just a dog that's hungry and hurt."

"No bear? A dog? Then—what's your name?" Chester asked, keeping his distance.

"Never had a name," the dog replied. "Except 'stupid' or 'mutt.'"

"Good gravy—every dog has to have a name, isn't that right, Kito?"

"Yup, every dog needs a name." He studied the dog and his shaggy, black coat. "Seems we could call you 'Bear.' What do you say to that?"

"Bear," the dog echoed.

"Can you follow us home?" Kito asked. "If you could, I'm certain you could sleep inside." He considered the dog's smell. "Or at least in the garage, and that's a lot warmer than here."

Bear tried to stand, then flopped back down again. "Can't," he said. "Ever since I was attacked by a moose."

"A moose!" Chester cried. "You've seen a moose?"

"Sure . . . beyond the village. Deer, wolves, moose, you name it. I've seen it."

"Criminy crackers!"

"I was so hungry, I started eyeing up a moose. Well, he tossed me with those antlers— flung me to the sky. I found my way here . . . somehow."

"Wow," Chester said. "Dog Watch would love to hear your story."

"If we don't get help for that wound," Kito said, "nobody will ever hear Bear's story— at least not from him. C'mon, Bear. You've gotta get outta here. You've gotta get moving."

Bear didn't move a smidgen.

"Chester, we need a plan. And Bear needs

more food." He turned to the moonlit entrance. "We'll be back just as soon as we can, Bear. You hang on, got it?"

Bear whimpered in reply.

12

End of Good Times

A branch cracked nearby as Kito and Chester crawled from Bear's den. Kito stopped. Had someone followed them?

"There you are!" Emmaline sang out.

With mittened hands, Zoey clapped. "We knew you dogs were up to something!" Chocolate and Snowball bounded after the girls. "When I saw so many dogs going this way from the sliding hill before, I said, 'Something's up,' didn't I, Emmaline?"

"You sure did!" In the moonlight, Emmaline

danced and skipped, sending sparkling snow-flakes into the air. "So what are you dogs up to?"

"Hey!" Chocolate said, clambering closer. "Whatcha doing?"

"Yeah, watcha doing?" Snowball repeated. "Wanna play?"

"Not now," Kito said.

The girls hurried after the puppies toward the dogs, closer and closer, as snow fluffed around their snow pants and boots.

"Hold your position," Kito whispered to Chester. "Block the opening to the den. They'll think we were just out playing in the snow."

"Right-o," Chester said, wiggling back-ward.

Chocolate tried to squirm between them. "Block what? I wanna see!"

"Yeah, we wanna see!" Snowball repeated.

"Get back," Kito warned with a growl.

At that, the puppies' tails drooped down and they backed up, cowering.

"You're hiding something," Emmaline

said, hands on her hips. "I just know it."

Zoey pulled dog biscuits from her jacket pocket. "Here, boys," she said, and the dogs all sprang to her side. The puppies fell all over themselves trying to get to the biscuits.

Kito caught the first biscuit, Chester the second, and the puppies searched for theirs in the snow.

"Oh, my gosh!" Emmaline cried out. "A den!"

"We blew it," Kito said, looking over his shoulder. The entrance to the den was wide open. "I can't believe we were duped so easily."

Emmaline knelt down and peered in.

"Careful!" Zoey warned. "It could be a wolf's den, or a bear's. . . ."

Emmaline jumped away, falling backward in the snow. She struggled to right herself.

From inside the den, Bear's whimpering turned to whining.

"Something's in there," Zoey said, standing taller and pushing her shoulders back. She squatted a short distance away, leaned her head down toward the snow, and peered into the den. "With the moon so bright," she said, "it's almost like a flashlight. I see a big—oh!"

Emmaline was back on her feet. "A wolf— I knew it! Let's run!"

Zoey held up her mittened hand. "No, not a wolf! It's a big dog, that's what it is. So that's what you dogs were doing out here. Maybe it has puppies, do you think?"

Kito shot Chester a disgusted look. "Puppies. Not quite."

Emmaline backed away. "Zoey, let's go get Mom and Dad. I'm sure there must be puppies in there."

"You're right. They won't be happy that we went to the hill after dark by ourselves, but we have to get help!"

Chocolate and Snowball tried to sneak into the den, but the girls caught them by their collars.

"Nope. You pups are coming with us."

Then the girls left, the snow quickly muffling their voices.

Again, Bear whimpered, his voice full of pain and sorrow, hunger and loneliness. Chester put his snout to the air, formed a round shape with his mouth, and started to howl a sad melody. "Whoooooooo-woo-woooooo!"

"Stop it," Kito said. He circled around Chester. "What are you doing?"

Chester stopped. "Bear just sounds so sad, it gets in my hound-bred bones. Makes me sing the blues."

"Oh, for the love of Pembrook. This isn't the time to sing. C'mon! We'd better follow the girls."

In moments they caught up to Emmaline and Zoey, then trotted with them all the way to the community building. Red lights framed the roof, a sleigh and reindeer of blue lights hung on the building, and outside, cars lined the street. The girls marched up the shoveled sidewalk to the entrance door and slipped inside, closing the door before Chocolate and Snowball could follow them. The puppies pressed their paws and noses to the windows and whined.

Chester and Kito stared inside. Across the polished wooden floor, rows of folding chairs were filled with Pembrook villagers. Standing before the audience were Petey's mother and short, round Mayor Jorgenson, who spoke through his red and white megaphone.

Mr. and Mrs. H sat in the back row beside Mr. and Mrs. Tweet. And behind them, Angelica Phillips stood tall, camera draped around her neck as she wrote on a notepad.

"I nearly forgot," Kito said, his voice heavy with dread.

"They're meeting about us, aren't they?" Chester said.

"What do you mean, 'us'?" Chocolate began jumping up and down, as if that might help him gain entrance.

Kito explained, "This is an emergency meeting to get all the dogs of the village on leashes forever."

"But why?" Snowball asked. "That's mean. Why?"

"Little buddies," Chester said, "sometimes life just isn't fair."

The dogs watched Emmaline and Zoey scoot in near their parents and whisper in their mom's ear. Mrs. Tweet whispered in Mr. Tweet's ear, who whispered in Mrs. H's ear, who whispered in Mr. H's ear. Then, as one, they rose from their seats and left the meeting. When they all stepped outside, Angelica Phillips followed with a curious tilt of her head.

The girls and the grown-ups stood clustered together. "Girls," Mrs. Tweet began. "What's going on?"

Soon, Angelica Phillips wiggled into the circle. "A den? I overheard—and forgive me for being nosy—but a den could mean many things. A bear, possibly. Could be an important story for the newspaper."

"No," Zoey explained. "It's a big dog, and it might have puppies in there."

"Another dog? Oh, just what we need!"

"Girls," Mr. and Mrs. H said, "we'll stop by home first with our dogs and then join you."

"We'll do the same with our puppies," agreed the Tweets.

And then, before Kito understood what was happening, the Tweets and the Hollinghorsts briefly headed home. The dogs followed. Chocolate and Snowball went with their family into their church-home. And Kito and Chester stepped inside their house across the street, right after Mr. and Mrs. H.

"Boys," Mrs. H explained, "we're sorry, and we don't expect you to understand, but until further notice—at least until after the holidays—all dogs have to be kept at home. Starting immediately."

"We don't agree with this decision," said Mr. H, "but rules are rules."

They patted the dogs on their heads, then stepped back outside into the snowy world. They met up with the neighbor family and set off again down the street, this time without dogs.

Kito pressed his nose to the cold glass of the door.

Chester stared outside. "I can't believe it. I just can't believe it."

"Fences, chains—leashes," Kito said. His whole body drooped until he was on the floor, head heavy on his paws.

Chester slumped on the floor beside him. "Criminy biscuits."

Kito closed his eyes in despair. "I feel positively sick. And now they're going to find Bear. What chance does he have now if Angelica Phillips pushes her nose into things?"

The Darkest Day of the Year

The sun dropped like a stone below the horizon. It was the shortest day of the year—December 21, the winter solstice—when the sun barely climbed above the treetops. If it weren't for the holiday lights, Kito thought he might curl up in a ball and die. Utterly depressed, he lay with Chester near the woodstove, his eyes closed.

One week had passed since the village meeting. Since then, every dog in the village had been forced to stay at home or on a leash. How could a dog go to the fire hydrant and share news with the rest of the dogs? No, they could share a glance from cars, see each other in passing when their owners took them for walks, and only occasionally touch noses if and when villagers decided to talk. Dog Watch had completely fallen apart. And every dog that Kito had seen hung his or her head and walked less briskly.

These were sad days, indeed, for Pembrook dogs.

"Worst of all," he said, letting Chester in on his thoughts, "tonight's the village Christmas party. Even if we're allowed to go, we'll be on leashes. No running up and down the hill, no working the warming house for cookies and treats. It's just not the same." He opened his eyes, rose to his legs, and stretched. "And I'm getting chubby with all this lying around."

"Good gravy, there's nothing wrong with that!" Chester said. "But it's weird. Here we left a half-dead, starving dog in its den and we have no idea what happened to him. Bear needed us, and we let him down. I hate to say it, but do you think he survived?"

"Emmaline and Zoey, once they led their mom and dad there, would have tried to help, but my guess is that Angelica Phillips would have called someone from the county Humane Society and had the dog shipped away to be put to sleep."

"Put to sleep—as in . . ."

"Don't say it," Kito said. "It's too awful to think about. Poor guy survived a moose attack. He must have started out as an abandoned puppy, left to scratch out a life for himself all alone. No wonder he raided the garbage cans at the warming house. He was starving!"

"Do you think he attacked Petey, really?"

"I've been thinking about that. From what I can piece together, I bet Bear was on his way to the den and Petey probably swooped right by him on the sled, scaring him to tears, that's all."

"Scaring Bear to tears?"

"No, Petey."

"Unless we hear someone talking about Bear, we'll never really know, will we?"

Kito walked to the door and looked out the glass at the snowy world beyond. "Nope."

Chester stood beside him. "It's all a diggity-dang shame."

Book in hand, Mr. H wound down the spiral stairs. "Oh, looks like you two want to go out." He put on his boots, then took them out one at a time and clipped them to the new system of cables. Two high cables, to which each dog was tethered, ran from the house to the shed.

"I'm sorry," said Mr. H. "I know this isn't the best, but I have to follow the new rules." Then he stepped inside and closed the door.

In the distance, a voice rose on the calm, frigid air. It was a dog's howl—it was Tundra! "Dog Watch!" she wailed. "Listen well!"

Kito and Chester perked up their ears. When dogs were too far apart to use silent language, then they had to howl and bark their messages.

"Time to protest!" she continued. "Time

to lift our voices until we're heard! We will protest until we're set free!"

Then, like a Christmas miracle, voices of dogs from every corner of the village—from north to south, from east to west—began to pick up the chorus.

"Protest!" came Schmitty's howl.

"Prooooooo-test!" Gunnar's voice rose from the direction of the tavern.

"Protest!" Muffin sang, her Southern drawl sweet to hear.

Chester threw his head and floppy ears back, lifted his snout, and shaped his mouth into a perfect O. Then he began to sing the blues. "Proootest, I mean, proootest!"

Everything in Kito—his disappointments, his sorrows, his sense of failure—it all changed and gathered into hope. He sat square on his haunches, raised his black nose to the gray sky, and howled like he'd never howled before. In fact, he never had howled before. This was a first! The howl went on and on, surging from his lungs to the sky, a soulful song, a cry for freedom.

"Protest! Protest! Freedom! Freedom!"

And soon all the Pembrook dogs were sitting outside, for no owner could put up with a howling dog indoors. Chained or fenced, they cried out as one: "FREEDOM! FREEDOM! FREEDOM! FREEDOM! . . ."

And they didn't stop, couldn't stop.

Next door, Mayor Jorgenson stepped out from his house. Bundled in his fur hat and parka, he called, "Kito! Chester! What's with all the noise out here?"

But they didn't stop, couldn't stop. The song they'd taken up came from their hearts, from everything that was good in them, and they howled all the louder. "FREEDOM!"

Mr. Jorgenson put his hands to his fur hat. "The dogs have gone crazy!"

Criminy Christmas!

As Kito and Chester howled at the sky, Mr. and Mrs. Hollinghorst stepped outside, dressed in their parkas. "Boys," Mrs. H said, "quiet down!"

Then they glanced up toward the sky, noticing the chorus of other dogs' voices. "Dear," Mr. H said, "what's going on?"

"Honey, I have no idea!"

Mr. Jorgenson trudged from his house through the snow to the Hollinghorsts' side. "What's going on indeed? Come with me, please. We better find out."

Chester and Kito howled from their backyard cables as the three set off down the village street, passing little Chocolate and Snowball, who were out on chains too, shivering, yet singing.

Before two hours had passed, everything changed. Mr. Jorgenson returned with the Hollinghorsts, who unclipped Kito and Chester from their tethers. Mr. and Mrs. H smiled.

Chester and Kito danced around their boots. "Yup," explained Mrs. H, "we went with the mayor to every door in Pembrook to convince villagers to reconsider. And so— you're free."

Chester nearly jumped to the sky. Kito rolled in the snow and shook his coat with a mini-snowstorm.

"It's almost like they understand," Mr. H said. He put his curved pipe to his mouth and lit it with a match. "Then again, maybe they do." He winked at his wife.

She motioned to the door. "The party

starts soon. I have to finish frosting a few gingerbread men."

Every dog and villager showed up at the warming house. The village Christmas party was on.

"Hi, hi, hi!" Howie greeted every person and dog who entered. A tiny Christmas tree sat on a table surrounded by wrapped gifts. Another table held an assortment of cookies and a pot of steaming cider.

With so much tail-wagging, a few cups tipped onto the floor, but no one seemed to get upset. Petey hovered near the gifts. His mother chatted with the mayor.

"Really, Mayor Jorgenson, I think we should reconsider . . ."

Kito smiled to himself. Dog Watch had worked. Together, the dogs had howled themselves free.

Schmitty, Lucky, and Gunnar came and went—in for snacks and handouts, then back out again to the hill. Muffin allowed herself to be carried in the arms of a teenage figure skater who twirled elegantly across the rink. "Woo-weee," Muffin called. "Ain't I some-thin'?"

The biggest surprise, however, came in the door later with Angelica Phillips. In a yellow parka and furry white boots, Angelica stopped in the middle of the warming house. She held up her hand.

Mr. and Mrs. H sat on a bench against the wall, and Kito and Chester sat beside them. "Trouble," Kito said. "I should have known this was all too good to be true."

Chester slunk under the bench. "Criminy Christmas!"

"Ahem," Angelica Phillips said, until the warming house silenced. Everyone looked her way. "I realize that I had something to do with cracking down on the dogs in Pembrook," she began. "And though I still have my doubts about dogs running free—there are always risks in that—I will try to be open-minded. I'm a newcomer, after all, from Chicago, and I'm learning that things are different here."

Kito felt his shoulders relax slightly. Was it possible for Angelica Phillips to soften, to see things differently? Maybe the magic of the season was working on her heart, too.

"And with that said," she continued, "I'd like to introduce you to the new love of my life." She stepped outside, then returned quickly with a big, black, burly dog at her side. "This is Bear."

Kito and Chester shot each other a questioning look. "How could she know his name is Bear?" Chester asked. "That's scary."

"Coincidence," Kito said, "pure and simple. I mean, look at him. He looks like a bear, doesn't he?"

Bear sat at her feet. A white bandage covered his wound. But his ribs were no longer visible. Already, in only a week's time, he'd put on some weight and his coat had taken on a slight sheen.

"Look at him," Kito said. "Amazing!"

Angelica Phillips knelt beside Bear, put her arms around his neck, and looked at

Petey. "Petey, I think this must be who you stumbled across when you were sliding in the woods. Come over and pet him. He's really a big teddy bear."

With his arms tightly at his sides, Petey glanced up at his mom, and then he cautiously made his way from the Christmas tree and gifts toward Bear's.

"Go ahead," Angelica said. "Pet him. He loves to be scratched under his chin."

Petey reached out, hesitated, then scratched Bear. In seconds the boy's face warmed to a confident smile. Bear licked Petey's hand.

"Bear," Angelica said, "was a homeless, starving dog, who until one week ago tried to survive in a hillside den. That's what the dogs in Pembrook had been after." She glanced around, resting her eyes on Kito. "Maybe, just maybe, they were gathering as a pack to get our attention—to tell us."

Kito could barely believe her change of mind.

"If not for Emmaline and Zoey," Angelica

Phillips continued, "who paid attention to the dogs, we would never have learned about Bear. He was injured—we'll never know how—and would have died. Died right under our noses in our own village." Tears budded in her eyes. She wrapped her arms around Bear's neck and burrowed her head into his fur. Then she took a deep breath, rose to her feet, and spoke. "So please welcome the newest dog, *my dog*, to Pembrook."

A thunderous sound of clapping broke out around the room. And from that moment on, the Christmas party was filled with good cheer, laughter, and treats. Villagers and dogs shared the rinks, the sliding hill, and the warming house.

Before everyone left for home, villagers exchanged gift-wrapped ornaments from under the tree. And yet a pile of small red packages with green bows remained. The villagers exchanged glances.

"Gifts for dogs," Howie explained, and handed the tiny packages out to the owners.

"It's for you, Chester," Mrs. H said. "It says, 'From Angelica Phillips.'"

Mr. H opened Kito's gift. "This is from her too. She must have given a gift to every dog in the village." Then Mr. and Mrs. H held up small rawhide bones shaped and colored like candy canes.

Kito and Chester gently received their gifts with their teeth.

And then the party was over. Kito trotted toward home with Chester and the Hollinghorsts, the Tweets and their puppies. Chocolate and Snowball darted back and forth between Chester and Kito, licking at the edges of their mouths and their chins. Normally Kito would bristle, but this night, he could feel nothing less than cheery goodwill, even for nuisance puppies.

Snow shimmered softly under streetlights. The girls laughed and talked, their voices soft and musical as wind chimes. From every house, Christmas lights sparkled brilliantly as jewels.

Kito breathed in the clean, crisp air. Dog Watch had helped save a dog in need. Villagers were getting along, and the dogs had won back their freedom. Once again, all was well in Pembrook.

There's trouble in town!

In the far north, winter left grudgingly.
By March, seagulls and pelicans returned,
waiting for the last snowfall to pass. In April
they floated on ice rafts under the trestle

bridge, as chunk by chunk, ice melted off the big lake. Villagers waited for spring too. In May the ice was finally gone. The start of the fishing season—or Fishing Opener—was only days away, and the village of Pembrook bustled with activity.

With the other village dogs, Kito and Chester gathered at the fire hydrant outside the post office. They met there every morning—all sniffs and wags—to catch up on recent news. The dogs had discussed how their owners were forgetting vet appointments, neglecting to walk their dogs, and missing regular feeding times. But this morning's talk was of a more serious nature.

"We were robbed!" Tundra exclaimed. "I'll never be able to hold my head high again."

Kito couldn't believe what he was hearing! Normally Tundra carried her white German shepherd body tall and proud as she circled the other dogs at the fire hydrant. As their leader, she enforced order and discipline, teeth to neck if necessary. But this morning was different.

Tundra's head hung low. She sat heavily on her haunches, waiting for her owner, Mr. Erickson, to pick up his mail. "Find a new alpha dog," she said, eyes cast toward the sidewalk. "I'm useless."

"But there must be an explanation," Kito said, squaring his chow shoulders and stepping closer. "Tundra, nobody gets past you!"

"Huh. Well, it looks like somebody has, Kito. Somebody certainly has."

"Criminy biscuits!" Chester exclaimed. "Tundra, just because you were robbed doesn't mean you throw in the beef bone, hide under the bed, run from the—"

"Chester, stop! I get your point, but it doesn't matter," she said. "What is a dog truly worth if it can't stop a burglar from robbing its own home?"

A sparkling purple truck towing a matching fishing boat roared past, right through a fresh rain puddle, splashing them all. Kito scowled and shook his coat. Strangers. A low growl vibrated in his throat. With the Fishing Opener just a few days away, lots of strangers were heading through Pembrook.